Seat 4F: Return Flight

by Honey Thomas

Seat 4F Return Flight

© 2025 Honey Thomas

This is a work of fiction. Names, characters, businesses, places, events, locales, and incidents are either the products of the author's imagination or used in a fictitious manner. Any resemblance to actual persons, living or dead, or actual events is purely coincidental.

ISBN: 978-1-7355974-5-4

Dedication

For every Black woman who's ever been told she was too much—

May you take up space, fall madly in love, and still chase your legacy.

This one's for you.

—Honey

Acknowledgments

To my readers—

Thank you for returning to Seat 4F. Your love made this story take flight again.

To my sisters in spirit, in hustle, and in heart—thank you for being my mirror, my muse, and my muscle.

To every woman building empires and still daring to be soft—you are proof that power and tenderness can coexist.

And to love itself—thank you for showing up, even when we're scared to receive it.

Special thanks to everyone who championed this sequel. You know who you are. Your belief kept me writing.

Table of Contents

Chapter 1 - Touch Down, Turned On   1

Chapter 2 - West Side Mornings, South Side Nights   6

Chapter 3 - Roof Top Vows & Champagne   11

Chapter 4 - Sunday Dinners & Soft Places   16

Chapter 5 - Another Woman's Name   20

Chapter 6 - Jealousy Looks Good on You   25

Chapter 7 - Love Don't Clock Out   29

Chapter 8 - Let's Build Here   34

Chapter 9 - Room for Forever   38

Chapter 10 - Couple Things   43

Chapter 11 - In the Mirror   48

Chapter 12 - Letters To Ourselves   52

Chapter 13 - The Yes Dress   57

Chapter 14 - Back to Where We Began   62

Chapter 15 - First Class Forever   67

Chapter 16 - The Engagement High   71

Chapter 17 - Bridal, Bougie & Boundaries   76

Chapter 18 - Meet Me at the Manor   80

Chapter 19 - The Softest Yes   84

Chapter 20 - Seat 4F – Full Circle   90

Bonus Epilogue: Return Flight   94

Chapter 1: Touch Down, Turned On

One year later

The Chicago skyline stretched across the window like a lover waiting to be touched. Raygen Porter leaned against the glass in her car, phone in one hand, lips glossed, eyes low and heavy from the flight—but her body? Her body was wide awake.

She was coming home.

But more than that—she was coming back to him.

D.C. had been a whirlwind. Speaking engagements, client pitches, and champagne receptions that looked good in pictures but felt like empty calories. Frank hadn't come this time. They'd agreed—he needed to close a local deal, and she needed to move on this brand expansion. Separate moves, same mission. But two weeks without him?

She felt it everywhere.

In the quiet at night.

In the way her fingers wandered between her thighs, but never finished.

In the ache behind her breastbone that only he knew how to press on.

The car slowed in front of his building.

She stepped out into the warm evening air, suitcase in tow, heels clicking with intention. The lobby guard gave her a knowing nod and buzzed her up without a word. As the elevator rose, her heart did the same.

When the doors opened, Frank was already there. Waiting.

One hand tucked in his pocket, jaw freshly shaved, his T-shirt stretched across a chest that still made her tongue press to the roof of her mouth. He didn't smile right away. Just watched her step into his space like she belonged there.

Then, low and rough: "Took you long enough."

Raygen dropped her bag, closed the space between them, and kissed him before she could say a word. Her hands found the back of his neck. His mouth met hers with a hunger that tasted like missed time and whispered need.

He backed her against the wall, his lips grazing her ear. "You been actin' busy. But I know you missed me."

Her voice was breathless. "I touched myself thinking about you last night."

He growled into her neck. "Bet it wasn't enough."

"It wasn't."

He grabbed her thigh, lifting her just enough for her legs to wrap around him.

"You wanna say hi to the bed," he murmured, "or you want the kitchen counter first?"

She bit his lip. "Wherever's closer."

The counter won.

Frank spun her around and bent her forward just slightly. Her fingers braced against the cool stone as his hands pulled her skirt up slowly. Her panties dropped to her ankles before she could gasp.

He took his time.

Fingertips dragging across the inside of her thighs. Mouth kissing the dip of her spine. When he slid inside her, she exhaled like she'd been holding that breath since she left.

Their rhythm was slow at first. Deep. Like a conversation between bodies that didn't need words. Then faster—hands gripping, moans rising, the air thick with sweat and possession.

Raygen reached back, fingers tangling in his. "I missed this," she moaned.

He leaned over, lips brushing her shoulder. "Say it louder."

She did.

And when she came, it was his name—sharp and sacred—ripping from her throat.

Later, wrapped in nothing but each other and the linen sheets, they lay tangled in the dim light of the bedroom.

"Tell me something," Raygen whispered, tracing a slow line along Frank's collarbone.

He looked down at her. "Yeah?"

"What were you thinking the second you saw me tonight?"

Frank ran his hand down the curve of her hip, squeezing gently. "That I should've booked your return flight myself. And put it for two days ago."

Raygen laughed, soft and satisfied. "I was thinking the same thing on night three."

Frank leaned in and kissed her slowly. "Don't leave me that long again."

"I won't," she promised, voice low. "Not unless you're on the plane with me next time."

He pulled her closer, tucked her head beneath his chin. "Deal."

They drifted off like that—heartbeats matching, legs tangled, peace wrapped around them like a blanket.

Outside, the city moved fast. But in here?

In here, time obeyed them.

Chapter 2: West Side Mornings, South Side Nights

Raygen didn't set an alarm that morning. Her body woke naturally, wrapped in golden sheets and Frank's arm heavy across her waist. The air smelled like him—clean skin, sleep, and quiet strength.

She turned carefully, watching his chest rise and fall. His lashes were thick. His mouth slightly parted. Vulnerable. Still. The kind of still you only showed to someone you trusted.

She kissed his shoulder and slid out of bed, her silk robe brushing over bare skin.

In the kitchen, sunlight spilled through the windows, lighting up the pale tile. She opened the fridge and grabbed the eggs, humming as she moved. Cooking wasn't really her thing—but showing up for him was.

She was just plating the last two pieces of toast when Frank walked in, shirtless and slow-moving.

"You cookin' now?" he asked, voice scratchy and sexy.

Raygen smiled over her shoulder. "Just making sure you don't fall apart without me."

He stepped behind her, wrapped both arms around her waist, and kissed her neck. "Too late for that."

They ate together on the balcony, legs brushing under the small table, city skyline in full view.

"So what's the plan today?" she asked, sipping orange juice.

Frank leaned back in his chair. "Thought I'd take you to the space I'm renovating."

"Oh? The warehouse?"

He nodded. "It's turning into something special. Community, commerce, culture. You'll see."

Raygen grinned. "And tonight?"

He smirked. "Whatever you want. You call the night shift."

Later that afternoon, they pulled into a quiet block on the South Side. It wasn't flashy, but it felt like legacy. Kids on bikes, old men posted on porches with cards and dominoes, aunties in slippers watering the sidewalk like it owed them money.

The warehouse Frank had mentioned sat at the corner. Brick exterior. Wide windows. Fresh paint already going up.

"Wow," Raygen whispered. "This used to be—"

"A storage spot," Frank finished. "Dead space. I bought the block. Flipping this into a multipurpose hub. Art, tech, youth development."

She looked at him, eyes soft. "You've been quiet about this."

"I don't build for cameras," he said. "I build for people."

They stepped inside. The air was cool, the walls bare but promising.

As he walked her through each section, describing plans—shared office space, indoor garden, a rooftop lounge—Raygen saw something in his face she hadn't seen before.

Purpose. Peace. Home.

When he finished the tour, he led her to the rooftop. No lounge furniture yet—just crates and a tarp—but the view?

Breathtaking.

Raygen sat on an overturned crate, legs crossed, eyes glowing.

"You got vision."

He looked at her, steady. "So do you."

Their eyes locked. There was a long pause. Then—

"You want to come with me to my auntie's house tomorrow?" she asked.

"West Side. Sunday dinner."

Frank tilted his head. "You sure they ready for me?"

Raygen smirked. "They might not be. But I am."

He reached for her hand. "Then it's a date."

That night, they drove to her place.

She led him in by the hand, kicked off her heels, and collapsed onto the couch.

Frank lay beside her. Quiet. Comfortable.

"I like your world," he murmured. "It feels warm."

Raygen smiled. "Yours feels big."

"They're gonna blend one day."

"You think so?"

He turned her chin toward him. "I know so."

She leaned in for a kiss, slow and unhurried. One of those deep ones that got under the skin. His hand slid beneath her shirt. Hers pushed past the waistband of his sweats. They didn't rush. They moved like people who knew they had time.

Later, in the dim light of her bedroom, their bodies moved together again. Softer this time. Slower. Less about hunger—more about holding.

No words. Just sighs. Skin. Trust.

And when they finally collapsed into each other, breathless and tangled, Raygen whispered:

"This feels too good."

Frank kissed her forehead.

"That's 'cause it's real."

Chapter 3: Rooftop Vows & Champagne

Frank didn't give her much to go on.

"Wear something soft," he said over the phone.

"Soft?" Raygen asked. "Like emotionally, or like silk?"

He just chuckled. "Both."

When the car pulled up that evening, her dress hugged like a second skin—thin straps, a low back, a color that made her look like sunset and satin. Her curls were swept up. Her lips barely glossed. No perfume. Just cocoa butter and confidence.

The building was unfamiliar—tall, modern, nestled on a quiet street in the South Loop. Frank met her at the entrance with a single key in hand and a look that made her thighs press together.

"Come on," he said, kissing her cheek. "It's up top."

The elevator opened onto a private rooftop.

Wide open sky. The hum of summer air. A table set

for two beneath a string of warm lights. Champagne chilling in a bucket. Soft music floating in the background. Her eyes widened.

"You did all this?"

Frank nodded. "You been moving nonstop. I figured we needed a night that wasn't about anything but you and me."

She turned slowly, taking it in. "This looks like a proposal setup."

He raised a brow. "You want it to be?"

Raygen laughed, cheeks flushed. "You're dangerous."

They ate dinner under the stars. Talked about music, favorite childhood snacks, and the kind of random dreams you rarely discuss out loud. Frank told her about his mom's laugh. Raygen told him how she used to cry in the bathroom before client meetings when she was just starting out.

There were no masks between them.

Just space. Just air. Just them.

He popped the champagne and poured it slowly. The bubbles spilled over her fingers. She licked the sweetness from her knuckle. His eyes tracked the movement like prey.

"You know," he said, leaning back in his chair, "I could get used to this."

Raygen smirked. "The view?"

With a slow shake of his head, one word escaped his lips. "You."

The silence that followed didn't need filling.

When the music shifted to something more profound, slower, Frank stood and held out his hand. "Come dance with me."

Raygen's fingers intertwined with his.

They moved together beneath the open sky, bodies pressed close. Her head rested against his chest. His fingers gripped her waist. There were no choreographed steps—just rhythm and desire and a thousand unsaid things.

"You ever think about where this is going?" she asked quietly.

"Every damn day," he replied.

"And?"

He pulled back just enough to meet her eyes. "And if you let me... I'll love you out loud, for real. No breaks. No guessing."

Raygen felt the words bloom inside her. Slow and soft and unshakable.

She reached up, kissed him—this time not with heat, but with truth.

They didn't make it back to the table.

Frank picked her up and carried her to the lounge area

tucked in the corner. Cushions, throws, soft lighting. He laid her down gently and climbed over her like he was coming home.

"You want this?" he asked, breath warm against her jaw.

"I need this," she whispered.

He moved like water over her skin—slow, smooth, deliberate. Unzipped her dress with one hand. Slid it off with reverence. Kissed the inside of her thighs like he was praying with his mouth.

Raygen gasped as he tasted her—slow licks, deep pressure, his fingers gripping her hips as if he'd never let go. Her hands were in his hair. Her legs trembled. And when she came, it was like something sacred had been pulled from her core.

He moved up her body, eyes locked with hers, and when he slid inside, they both exhaled like the world had gone quiet.

They moved together—soft grinds, deep strokes, slow passion. The wind wrapped around them. Their moans danced with the breeze.

His name.

Her hands.

The sky.

It was the kind of night you don't forget even when you're old and gray, still pretending you never had sex on

14

a rooftop.

Later, they lay beneath a throw blanket, her head on his chest, fingers tracing the lines of his tattoo.

Raygen whispered, "What would you have done if I said yes earlier?"

"To what?"

"When you joked about a proposal."

Frank kissed her temple.

"I would've dropped to my knees right then. No ring. Just heart."

Raygen blinked slowly.

"Good thing you didn't," she teased. "Or I might've said yes."

He looked down at her. "Might?"

She smiled, eyes fluttering closed. "Ask me again one day."

"I will."

Chapter 4: Sunday Dinners & Soft Places

"You sure you wanna do this?" Raygen asked, adjusting her earrings in the passenger seat.

Frank glanced at her hand resting on the gearshift. "Why wouldn't I?"

She gave him a look. "You ever had to explain to six aunties at once why your cologne smells expensive and your hands look too soft to change a tire?"

He laughed. "I've been in boardrooms with million-dollar egos and fake smiles. A house full of women who love you? That's light work."

Raygen smirked, nervous but hiding it well. "Mmm. Don't say I didn't warn you."

They pulled up to a small bungalow on the West Side—brick, modest, with a porch full of plants, wind chimes, and folding chairs. You could smell the greens from the sidewalk. Laughter and gospel music poured out from the screen door.

As they walked up, Raygen held Frank's hand a little tighter.

"Stick close," she whispered.

Inside was exactly what she promised—tight hugs, loud voices, cluttered counters, and soul food in every direction. Her Aunt Vi was at the stove with a wooden spoon like it was a weapon.

"Well, well, well," she said, turning with one eyebrow raised. "You must be the man taking up all my niece's FaceTime minutes."

Frank grinned and extended his hand. "Nice to meet you, Ma'am."

"Mmm," Vi said, shaking it. "He got manners."

"He also brought peach cobbler," Raygen added.

Aunt Vi smirked. "Oh, he tryin' to stay."

Dinner was a full-on cultural event.

Plates stacked high. Jokes flying. Frankie Beverly hummed through the Bluetooth speaker. The grown-ups played dominoes at the card table. The kids ran through the house as if it were an obstacle course. And Frank? He fit in like he'd been there before.

He helped clear plates. Talked real estate with Raygen's uncle. Laughed loud when her cousin roasted him for eating seconds before everyone was done.

Raygen watched him with quiet pride, her gaze sparkling and steady.

He wasn't putting on. He was present.

And when he leaned over and whispered in her ear, "This your origin story, huh?" she smiled widely.

"This is my soft place," she said.

Later, as the sun dipped low and the porch lights came on, Raygen and Frank sat outside on the swing while the night cooled.

"I didn't expect to like this so much," he admitted. "Usually, family settings feel like a setup."

Raygen leaned into him. "That's 'cause they usually are."

Frank chuckled. "Nah, this felt... familiar. My people didn't do the big gathering thing. We moved too much. This was real."

Raygen looked up at him. "I want more of this."

"You'll have it."

"With you?"

Frank turned toward her. "Ray, I want a future that feels like this. You, me, love that doesn't have to perform. Just real."

She was quiet for a long beat.

Then she kissed his shoulder. "Don't say things like that unless you mean them."

"I don't say anything I don't mean."

Their eyes locked in the porch light. No noise. No cameras. Just two people being seen.

He kissed her slow. No urgency. Just truth.

Her fingers slid up his jawline. "You ever think… this is what people mean when they say home?"

Frank nodded. "Yeah."

Then he whispered, "And you feel like mine."

They left with takeout plates and full hearts. Back at her place, they didn't rush.

He undressed her like it were an act of gratitude.

She touched him like his body was a language she wanted to relearn.

The sex that night was slow, rich, worshipful.

No games. No teasing. Just love—loud and undeniable.

And when they fell asleep wrapped around each other, Raygen whispered into the dark:

"I've never been loved like this."

Frank, half asleep, replied:

"You've never been loved by me."

Chapter 5: Another Woman's Name

Raygen never went through Frank's phone.

She didn't need to. Didn't want to. That kind of love—the anxious, nosey kind—was for people who'd been betrayed. She wasn't trying to build her future off suspicion.

But that morning, she was reaching for her charger on the nightstand when Frank's phone lit up with a missed call.

She saw the name before she could look away.

Simone.

That's all it said. First name. Nothing else.

Raygen didn't freeze. Didn't panic. Just… paused.

She stood there blinking, charger cord in hand, a quiet pull stirring in her chest. A flicker of doubt—not heavy, but sharp. Not because she thought he was cheating. But because she realized… Simone from St. Thomas was Frank's past.

And this? This name? Familiar in a way she couldn't explain.

Frank walked in moments later with two cups of hot tea.

"You good?" he asked, handing her a cup.

Raygen turned slowly. "Do I need to worry about Simone?"

Frank blinked once. Caught off guard, but not defensive.

"She's... someone I used to talk to. Before you. I thought you and I had passed this."

Raygen nodded once. "Used to?"

"Again. It was short. Complicated. Never turned into anything. I haven't seen her in over a year. Then I, we, saw her in St. Thomas."

Raygen folded her arms. "So why is she calling now?"

Frank exhaled, rubbing the back of his neck. "I don't know. Haven't talked to her since Saint Thomas."

There it was—the unknown.

Raygen looked away. Silent.

"I didn't think she mattered anymore."

The silence between them stretched.

Raygen walked into the kitchen, needing space. She

wasn't mad. Not really. But that name? It scraped at something within her. Not jealousy. Not fear. Something older.

A memory of being "the one after." A rebound. An almost.

Frank followed her slowly. "Ray. Talk to me."

She turned, leaning on the counter. "It's not her. It's the fact that I didn't know she existed. That someone from your past has access to you—still—and I wouldn't have known until now."

"I didn't hide her," Frank said. "But you're right. I should've told you in our many open conversations."

Raygen studied him. "Is she still in love with you?"

He didn't answer right away.

"I don't know."

Wrong answer.

Raygen picked up her tea, walked past him, and sat on the couch.

Frank sat across from her. "You ever have a moment where you realize how much someone means to you because something threatens it?"

She didn't speak.

"I'm not keeping anything from you," he said. "But I haven't told you everything either. Maybe because I didn't want to bring any weight from before into this."

Raygen looked at him.

"This is real to me, Frank. And if I'm building something with you, I need the full picture. Not the Instagram version. The scars. The regrets. The exes."

Frank nodded. "Okay."

"I'm serious."

"So am I."

A pause.

"Want me to call her?" he asked. "Right now? On speaker?"

Raygen blinked. "What?"

"I don't owe her anything. But I owe you clarity."

Raygen sat back. "No. That's unnecessary."

Frank leaned forward. "Then let me say this once— whatever she was, whoever she is, it ended a long time ago. You're my now. You're my next. You're the one."

Her eyes softened, but she wasn't all the way there yet.

"I'm not trying to control you," she said quietly.

"You're not. You're protecting something you care about. That's love."

Raygen sighed. "I just… needed to hear you say it."

Frank stood, walked to her, and pulled her gently to her feet.

"You feel how close I am to you?"

He pressed his forehead to hers.

"You feel how locked in I am?"

She nodded.

"Then trust me. We don't leave each other over shadows. We turn the lights on."

That night, Frank made love to her like he had something to prove—but not in a way that felt desperate. In a way that felt like anchoring. Like reminding her whose name he whispered when the world was quiet.

Raygen melted beneath him, beneath the rhythm of his mouth, the weight of his hands, the quiet groans he gave when she pulled him deeper.

She let him in.

Let the moment soothe the sting.

And when they were both breathless and spent, she whispered against his neck:

"I'm not going anywhere."

Frank kissed her shoulder. "Good. 'Cause neither am I."

Chapter 6: Jealousy Looks Good on You

The venue was packed.

A dimly lit lounge in River North, full of rising creatives, polished entrepreneurs, and the type of people who network by flirting. Raygen moved through the room like she belonged there—because she did. Confident, calm, dressed in a fitted two-piece that hugged every part of her just right.

Frank trailed slightly behind her, giving her space to shine. He loved watching her work a room—how she could make eye contact, listen deeply, flash that subtle smile that made people lean in without realizing it.

But tonight, someone leaned in a little too far.

Raygen was talking with a panel organizer near the bar when a tall man in a gray turtleneck slid in from the side. Too close. Too familiar. His voice low, flirty, hand lingering a second too long when he touched her arm.

Frank clocked it from ten feet away.

Raygen, ever poised, gave a tight smile. She was handling it. Still, something in Frank's jaw flexed.

He walked over just as the man said, "If you ever want to grab dinner—strictly creative convo, of course—I'd love to pick your brain."

Raygen opened her mouth to respond, but Frank was already at her side.

"She's busy tonight," he said, voice low and calm. "But thanks for the offer."

The man blinked, processing.

Raygen didn't look at Frank. She looked at the other guy and smiled, all teeth and no warmth. "Appreciate the compliment. But I'm very much… spoken for."

Frank wrapped an arm around her waist.

The man nodded, mumbled something polite, turned and began chatting with a woman at the bar.

Raygen sipped her drink slowly. "You handled that smoothly."

Frank leaned down, lips near her ear. "That wasn't smooth."

"Oh?"

"That was me not flipping a table."

Raygen laughed. "You jealous?"

He didn't smile. "Very."

She turned into him slightly. "Good."

They didn't even say goodbye to the room.

By the time they made it back to his place, Frank had her pressed against the front door before it could close.

"You let him touch your arm," he said, his voice low, lips grazing her jaw.

"I didn't let him. He touched it."

"You didn't stop him."

Raygen smirked, breath catching as his hand slid up the back of her thigh. "You mad?"

He lifted her in one motion, carried her across the room, laid her down on the couch like a gift he was about to unwrap.

"I'm not mad," he said, dragging his mouth along her collarbone. "I just want to remind you who makes you melt."

And then he did.

Frank took his time, undressing her like she was silk he didn't want to wrinkle. He kissed her thighs, licked the inside of her knee, worked his way up until she was moaning his name without shame. When he finally slid into her, it was deep, slow, and full of heat that bordered on reverence.

Raygen clung to him, nails digging into his back, legs locked tight around his waist.

"You like that?" he growled.

"Yes—don't stop."

"I wasn't planning to."

He flipped her over in a quick fierce motion, pressing her chest to the couch cushions, his hands gripping her hips as he drove into her deeper. Each stroke was a reminder. A claiming. A vow whispered through sweat and sighs.

When they finished, breathless and tangled, lying on their sides, he pulled her into his lap from behind, kissed her shoulder, and whispered, "Let 'em try you. Just know, they'll never know you like I do.

Raygen leaned back against him, lips parted, body glowing.

"Jealousy looks good on you," she whispered

"So does this sweat," he murmured, pulling her closer.

They sat like that in silence—his hands on her skin, her body humming from the aftershocks.

Chapter 7: Love Don't Clock Out

Raygen stared at the email longer than necessary.

The subject line glowed on her laptop screen:

"Official Offer – Executive Residency, New York City."

It was everything she'd worked for. Six months at a nationally recognized institute. A chance to scale her brand, consult across industries, rub shoulders with names she once wrote on her vision board. All expenses paid. Prestige. Power.

But it also meant one thing:

Leaving.

She clicked the email open, reread the details. Then closed her laptop with a quiet exhale and reached for her tea.

Later that evening, Frank walked in with groceries in one arm and takeout in the other.

"You cookin' and still brought food?" Raygen asked, kissing his cheek.

"Nah. The groceries are for tomorrow. The takeout is the real play."

She smiled but didn't really laugh.

He clocked it. "You good?"

"Yeah." A pause. "Mostly."

They sat on the couch, containers open between them, music low in the background.

Raygen played with her fork. "I got an offer today."

Frank looked up midbite. "Yeah?"

She nodded. "Executive residency. New York. Six months. Starts in the fall."

The room quieted. Not heavy. Just... still.

Frank leaned back. "Damn. That's big."

"It is."

"You gonna take it?"

Raygen looked at him, trying to read his expression. "I don't know. It's an incredible opportunity."

"It sounds like it."

Another pause. Too long.

Raygen set her food down. "Say what's on your mind, Frank."

He sighed, stretching his legs out. "I don't want to be the reason you don't grow. But I'd be lying if I said I want you gone for half a year."

She nodded, slow. "I figured."

"I mean, we just got into this rhythm," he said. "Us. Here. Now."

Raygen rubbed her hands together. "But we also said we wouldn't get in the way of each other's elevation."

"I meant that," Frank said. "But real talk? I didn't think elevation would mean a time zone."

She leaned into the couch. "Do you think we couldn't handle it?"

"I think we could. I just don't want to."

Raygen looked at him. "What if I said I want to go?"

Frank looked her dead in the eyes. "Then I'll fly out. Every other week. You say the word—I'll make it work."

That stopped her.

She tilted her head. "You would?"

"I'm not letting a zip code shrink what we have. Love don't clock out just because the office is in a different city."

Raygen blinked, heart suddenly tight in her chest. "You say that like you mean it."

"I do," he said. "But I also want to be honest. I don't want to need to prove how supportive I can be. I want us building together."

She moved closer, touched his jaw. "So then, what's the play?"

Frank pulled her onto his lap. "You do you. Take the offer. If it feels right."

"And you?"

"I'll be here. Or there. Or wherever you are. Just don't shut me out while you level up."

Raygen wrapped her arms around him, held him tight.

"I've never had this," she whispered. "This kind of love."

"Now you do."

They didn't make love that night, like usual.

There was no hunger. No rush.

Just slow undressing. Foreheads touching. His hand in hers as he kissed her chest, her belly, the inside of her wrist. She cried a little, without meaning to.

He kissed her tears.

Not to erase them.

But to say, I see you.

They lay in bed after, limbs tangled.

Frank whispered, "You're gonna kill it. Wherever you go."

Raygen kissed his chest. "You're home. I'll always come back."

Chapter 8: Let's Build Here

The morning air was crisp, sunlight streaking through the blinds in golden slices. Raygen stretched in bed, wearing nothing but Frank's oversized T-shirt. She could hear him in the other room—on the phone, voice low, serious.

When he came back in, he kissed her shoulder, whispered, "Get dressed. I want to show you something."

No questions. Just curiosity.

They drove west for nearly forty minutes, out of the noise, into something quieter. Trees. Space. The type of place where birds weren't just background—they were part of the soundtrack.

Frank pulled into a long driveway that led to a plot of land. Grassy. Open. Framed by trees. A little wild, but beautiful.

Raygen stepped out of the car slowly. "What is this?"

Frank handed her a manila envelope.

Inside: blueprints.

Her brows furrowed. She turned her eyes from the drawings to him. "This a project?"

He shook his head. "This is our project."

Raygen blinked. "Wait—ours?"

Frank nodded, stepping closer. "I've been working with an architect. I told him I wanted something that felt like us. Bold. Warm. Real. Room for people. Room for privacy. Room to grow."

Raygen flipped through the pages. "There's a reading nook."

"You always said you wanted one."

"And a soaking tub," she whispered.

Frank smiled. "Two, actually. One in the guest suite. You know how your aunties like to stay over."

Raygen looked up, heart stuttering. "You did all this... for me?"

"For us," he said, voice steady. "I know New York's calling. And if you go, I'll support that. But when you come home—if you want this to be home—I want you to know there's space for you. Not just in my life. In my foundation."

Raygen let the papers fall to her side. "Frank... I don't even know what to say."

He stepped close, took her face in both hands. "Say you see it."

She nodded. "I see it."

"Say you want it."

"I want it."

Then he kissed her—deep and full of promise.

They explored the land hand in hand. He pointed out where the kitchen would go, the deck, the room for future babies she hadn't even said she wanted yet. But the way he said, "'our kids one day'" made her toes curl in her boots.

Later, back in the car, Raygen sat with the blueprints in her lap. She wasn't crying, but her chest felt full in a way that almost hurt.

Frank watched her.

"I'm not trying to pressure you."

"You're not," she said softly. "You're loving me like I didn't know I needed."

That night, they didn't even make it to the bedroom.

Raygen straddled him on the couch, her nails scraping his scalp as she kissed him with every unspoken word.

"You want this?" she whispered.

"More than anything."

She rocked against him, slow and steady, grinding until his breath was ragged. He peeled her clothes off as if they were wrapping paper, kissed every inch of her, laying claim.

Their bodies moved like a language only they understood—rhythmic, reverent, raw.

When she rode him, it wasn't just sex.

It was submission to the moment. To the future.

To the fact that no matter what zip code she ended up in... she had already found home.

Chapter 9: Room for Forever

"This the one?" Raygen asked as Frank unlocked the front door.

"Nah," he said with a smirk, "but it is built on a similar blueprint. Figured we could spend a night here. Get a feel for it."

They stepped inside.

Warm lighting. Clean lines. Open concept. Big windows with soft evening light pouring through them. It was staged to feel like a life already lived—cozy throw blankets, half-open cookbooks, candles by the soaking tub. Someone's dream. Maybe theirs.

Raygen walked in slowly, heels echoing on the hardwood. "This already feels like us."

Frank kicked off his shoes, tossing his keys on the counter. "That's what I was hoping you'd say."

She turned, leaning against the kitchen island. "You

planned a whole little 'test drive' for domestic life?"

He stepped closer. "Something like that."

Their eyes met. Heat flickered.

Raygen grinned. "And what exactly are we testing tonight? The oven? The water pressure? Or how good this floor feels on our backs?"

Frank laughed, low and deep. "All the above."

They started in the kitchen. Frank pulled out a bottle of wine and poured them each a glass.

"Imagine this," he said, standing behind her, arms wrapped around her waist. "You comin' home from some major brand launch, kick your shoes off, and I'm in here making pasta—sauce from scratch, of course."

Raygen leaned into him. "You making sauce now?"

"I could be taught."

She laughed. "I'd marry you just for the effort."

There it was.

The word.

She felt his breath still for a second behind her.

"Say that again," he said, voice low.

Raygen turned slowly, lips brushing his. "I said what I said."

They didn't make it past the hallway.

Frank lifted her onto the console table by the stairs, kissed her so deeply she forgot where she was. Her thighs spread instinctively. His hands slid beneath her dress, slow and steady. She moaned against his mouth.

He carried her to the bedroom as if she weighed nothing and laid her down. He didn't rush.

Dress off. Lips trailing. Her hands sliding down his chest, undoing his shirt like she was unwrapping a gift.

"I want this every day," he murmured. "Waking up to you. Falling asleep next to you. Fighting about what color to paint the guest room."

Raygen smiled, lips parting as he kissed his way down her body. "And what if I want a reading room instead?"

"Then you'll get both."

He slipped inside her with a groan, deep and full, her back arching off the mattress. They moved slowly at first, savoring. Then faster. Hotter. Her legs wrapped tight around him, her breath catching with every stroke.

"Frank," she gasped. "Right there—don't stop."

"I'm not," he grunted. "You feel too damn good."

He flipped her onto her stomach, pulled her hips up. Entered her again from behind, deep and deliberate. His hand slid around to find her sweet spot. Her body trembled.

"You gonna come for me, baby?"

"Yes—yes, I'm—" She broke off with a cry.

He didn't stop. Kept pushing. Kept whispering.

"You mine?"

She nodded.

"Say it."

"I'm yours."

He kissed her spine. "Forever?"

She turned her head, eyes glazed. "Forever."

They lay in the aftermath, slick and breathless, tangled in the sheets of a home that didn't belong to them—yet.

Raygen rested her head on his chest. "I know this was just a model home... but it felt real."

Frank stroked her back. "That's 'cause it's real."

He reached over to the nightstand and pulled something out of a small drawer.

A velvet pouch.

He didn't open it.

Just laid it on her stomach and said, "When the time's right... this is yours."

Raygen blinked.

"Frank..."

"I'm not asking right now," he said. "I just want you to know where I'm headed."

41

She held the pouch, quiet. Then smiled.

"Good," she whispered. "Because I was already on my way there too."

Chapter 10: Couple Things

"You sure about this?" Raygen asked, brushing invisible lint off Frank's shoulder.

He glanced down at her with a smirk. "Too late to back out now."

The youth center buzzed behind them. A group of young adults—mostly twenty-somethings from the South and West Sides—were filtering into the workshop room. Fresh fades, fresh notebooks, and fresh energy. Some looked hungry. Some looked skeptical. All looked curious.

Raygen glanced at the banner hanging behind the projector screen.

"Six-Figure Starters: Building Wealth from the Ground Up"

Hosted by Frank Sheldon & Raygen Porter.

Frank funded the whole thing—venue, resources, stipends for attendees. But he made it clear: "This ain't charity. It's an investment."

Raygen adjusted her mic. "Okay. Let's light 'em up."

The room filled quickly. Frank kicked off the session with a story about flipping one property into ten without touching a bank loan. Raygen followed with her journey of turning one idea and $500 into a thriving lifestyle brand.

They didn't talk at the group—they talked to them.

They answered questions. Checked egos. Gave real numbers. Real mistakes. Real wins.

And they didn't always agree.

"Marketing is the game-changer," Raygen insisted, pacing in heels, full of fire. "If they don't know you exist, they won't buy a thing."

"True," Frank said, leaning against the table. "But you can market trash, and it'll still smell like trash. Product quality comes first."

They locked eyes.

She grinned. "I love when you try to check me in public."

He chuckled. "You love being wrong in public."

The room laughed, eating it up.

But beneath the banter was chemistry—undeniable and magnetic. You could feel it. They weren't just giving advice. They were giving an example.

After the final Q&A, the attendees lingered—taking selfies, asking more questions, thanking them.

One girl, maybe nineteen, walked up to Raygen with tears in her eyes.

"I didn't know women like you existed."

Raygen's throat tightened. She hugged her gently. "We do. And now that you know, go be one."

Later that night, the building was quiet. Lights low. Just the two of them packing up materials and wiping down whiteboards.

Frank leaned on the table. "You killed that."

Raygen smiled, stacking folders. "You weren't so bad yourself."

"Think we make a good team?"

She looked up. "Is that a trick question?"

He crossed the room in two steps, backed her against the wall, hands on either side of her waist.

"Because I've been thinking about our next project."

"Oh, yeah?" she whispered.

"Yeah. Starts in the back office. Ends with me tasting how proud I am of you."

She pulled him down by the collar. "Then don't waste time with small talk."

The back office door clicked shut.

Frank lifted her onto the desk without a word.

Kissed her like the day had been foreplay. Her blouse came off first. His shirt next. He sucked her bottom lip, then slid down, kissing between her breasts, along her ribs, down her belly.

Raygen gasped as he dropped to his knees, parted her thighs, and feasted like a man starved. Tongue slow, fingers precise, hands gripping like he'd die if she pulled away.

She came fast, sharp, loud.

But he wasn't done.

He stood, slid inside her, and groaned deep in her ear. "Still mine?"

"All yours," she moaned, wrapping her legs around him.

He moved deep, relentless, her back arched off the desk, their rhythm as tight as their teamwork had been hours ago.

"You think those kids noticed how good we are together?" she panted.

Frank smirked, kissing her neck. "We gave 'em something to look up to."

They left late. Smiling. Sore. Satisfied.

Raygen looked over at him in the parking lot. "Today was good.

Frank laced his fingers with hers. "Today was us."

Chapter 11: In the Mirror

The house was quiet.

No calls. No meetings. No Frank.

Just Raygen, a half-eaten croissant, and sunlight bleeding across her hardwood floors. Her heels sat untouched by the door. She was barefoot, in a loose robe, hair tied up, sipping coffee that had gone cold.

She sat on the edge of the bed, staring at herself in the mirror.

Not the curated version—the real one. No gloss. No filter. Just skin and silence.

She saw it all.

The woman who once second-guessed every move.

The one who used to bend herself small for approval.

The one who now walked into rooms like she belonged there… but still had moments like this.

Moments where fear crept in without knocking.

Because loving Frank this deeply?

It was terrifying.

He hadn't asked her to shrink. He hadn't made her question her worth. He held her, listened to her, touched her, like she was sacred.

And somehow, that scared her more than the heartbreaks before him.

Because if she lost this—it wouldn't just hurt.

It would unmake her.

Later, she FaceTimed Jasmyn.

"You ever love somebody so much it makes you nervous?"

Jasmyn didn't hesitate. "Hell yeah."

Raygen laughed, but her eyes were shiny.

"I just… feel like I'm waiting for the other shoe to drop."

"Ray," Jasmyn said gently, "you not scared of Frank. You scared of what it means to be safe. You've never had this much security and still been allowed to be soft."

Raygen was quiet.

"But that man sees you. And he ain't blinkin'."

That evening, Frank came home early.

He found her on the balcony, curled up with a book she wasn't really reading.

He walked up behind her, slid his arms around her shoulders, and kissed her temple.

"You good?" he asked, voice low and soft.

She nodded.

He didn't press. Just sat beside her, pulled her close.

After a long stretch of silence, she finally said, "Sometimes I wonder if I'm built for this kind of love."

Frank didn't flinch. "Why?"

"Because I've always been the strong one. The solo act. The one who bounced back. And now… I don't want to bounce. I just want to land. But that feels risky."

Frank reached for her hand, intertwining their fingers.

"Then land, baby," he whispered. "I'm not movin'."

Her throat tightened.

"I mean it," he said. "You don't gotta hold it together every day. You don't have to be perfect to be loved here."

Raygen leaned into his chest. Closed her eyes.

"Thank you," she whispered.

They didn't have sex that night. They just lay together, skin to skin, his hand tracing the length of her spine, her thumb softly strumming his bicep.

Sometimes love wasn't fireworks.

Sometimes it was this:

Quiet.

Still.

Safe.

Chapter 12: Letters to Ourselves

Frank drove with one hand on the wheel and the other resting on Raygen's thigh. The windows were down, music low, and the city slowly faded behind them as the trees grew taller and the roads got quieter.

Raygen looked out at the winding road, her curls dancing in the breeze. "You ever think about just... disappearing?"

Frank glanced over, smirking. "With or without you?"

She laughed. "Definitely with."

He squeezed her leg gently. "Then yeah. I think about it all the time."

They pulled up to a small lakefront cabin—modern, tucked into the woods, quiet in a way Chicago could never be. No service. No distractions. Just air and space.

Inside, the cabin was all wood and warmth. Tall windows. A stone fireplace. A deck that overlooked still water and trees that moved like secrets.

They cooked dinner together, barefoot, wine flowing, music humming in the background. Nothing fancy. Just pasta and garlic bread and the type of laughter that felt earned.

Afterward, they sat on the floor by the fireplace, wrapped in a blanket, sipping red wine.

Raygen looked over at him. "Wanna play a game?"

Frank raised an eyebrow. "You tryna lose again?"

She nudged him. "No. This is different."

She pulled out two pieces of paper and two pens from her bag.

"We write each other a letter," she said. "One rule— you have to say something you've never said out loud."

Frank leaned back. "You came prepared."

"I stay ready."

He smiled. "Alright then."

They sat quietly, the fire crackling, pens moving.

Frank went first.

He cleared his throat, unfolded the page.

Ray,

I didn't know how to love without holding back until you. Before you, I always kept one foot out the door. Not because I wanted to leave, but because I didn't trust that I was enough to be stayed for.

You changed that. I still get scared sometimes. Not of loving you—but of how much I need to love you right.

You deserve softness. Stability. And sometimes I question if a man who built himself from concrete knows how to give that.

But I'm learning. For you, I'm learning.

And I swear, I'm not going anywhere.

Raygen blinked fast, lips pressed together.

Frank reached for her hand, but she was already unfolding her letter.

Frank,

I used to be proud of how hard I was. How fast I could leave. How little I expected.

But now?

Now I want more. With you.

I want holidays. Arguments we get over in the same room. Waking up and knowing that even if we don't have everything figured out—we're figuring it out together.

You make me feel like I don't have to perform.

Just be.

And that... is the scariest, safest feeling I've ever known.

Silence.

Then Frank reached for her, pulled her into his lap, and held her for a long time.

"You good?" he asked softly, lips brushing her temple.

Raygen nodded. "I'm good. Better than good."

Later that night, they stood on the deck under a sky full of stars.

Raygen in a robe. Frank in sweats. The wind, soft and warm.

She turned to him. "Read me again."

He stepped behind her, pressed his lips to her ear.

"You changed that," he whispered. "For you, I'm learning."

She turned, took his face in both hands. Kissed him like his words were still on her tongue.

The robe fell first.

Then the silence.

Then everything else.

They made love slow that night—outside, under the stars, the wood planks of the deck warm beneath their bodies. Every touch said: I see you.

Every kiss said: Stay.

And every moan that slipped into the night sky became part of something bigger than sex.

It was worship.

It was love.

Chapter 13: The Yes Dress

"I'm not trying anything on," Raygen said, arms crossed as she stepped into the boutique.

Jasmyn rolled her eyes. "Girl, relax. It's my fitting. You're just here for support."

Raygen narrowed her eyes at the rows of white and ivory and blush hanging like dreams on velvet hangers. The room smelled like florals and fantasy. Mirrors everywhere. Champagne waiting in glass flutes.

Raygen grabbed one. "If I even breathe too hard, one of these dresses gon' jump on me."

"You sound scared," Jasmyn teased.

"I'm not scared. I just know what I want."

"Mmhmm."

As Jasmyn disappeared into the fitting room, the bridal consultant floated by with a smile. "Would you like to browse while you wait?"

Raygen shook her head.

Then paused.

A dress caught her eye. It wasn't poufy. No tulle. No rhinestones screaming for attention. It was sleek. Off-the-shoulder. Fitted in the bodice, flowing at the hip. Understated. Regal. Grown.

Her fingers brushed the fabric before she could stop herself.

"You wanna try it?" the consultant asked, gently.

Raygen hesitated. "...One minute won't hurt."

Ten minutes later, she stood in front of the mirror.

The dress hugged her perfectly. Her skin glowed. Her waist looked snatched. Her arms elegant. But it was the feeling that stopped her.

She looked like somebody's wife.

She looked like his.

She stood motionless in the mirror, gazing at the wedding dress adorning her, enraptured, lost in a dreamy trance.

Raygen exhaled, heart suddenly thudding in her ears.

And that's when the door opened.

Frank stepped in.

"Jas told me where you were—" His voice cut off mid-sentence.

He froze.

She turned slowly, eyes wide, caught.

Frank blinked, lips parted slightly. Then shut the door behind him and locked it.

"You good?" he asked, voice low.

Raygen nodded, unable to find words.

He walked to her slowly, his eyes never leaving hers. "That's the one."

"It's not mine," she blurted. "I just tried it for fun."

He stopped in front of her. "Nah. That's the one."

She swallowed hard. "You think so?"

Frank reached out, traced a finger along her collarbone. "I've never wanted to marry somebody so bad in my life."

Her breath hitched.

He stepped closer, eyes dark now. "You in that dress?"

"Yeah?"

"I need you out of it."

They didn't make it to the car.

Frank pulled her into the boutique's backroom, shutting the curtain behind them.

His hands were already on her, unzipping the dress, kissing her neck, her shoulder, the middle of her back. She gasped when his fingers found her center—wet, needy, already pulsing.

"You knew what you were doin'," he murmured, sliding two fingers inside her. "Tryin' this on. Lookin' like that."

"I didn't—mean to—" she moaned.

He dropped to his knees. Lifted one leg onto a chair.

"You gonna be my wife?"

"Yes," she gasped. "Frank—yes."

His tongue was on her before she could finish.

She clutched the curtain, head thrown back, trying not to scream as he licked and sucked her into oblivion. When she came, it was his name that filled the air, not wedding bells.

He stood, turned her around, lifting her easily.

"Right here?" she whispered, breathless.

"Right here," he growled.

He pushed inside her slowly, fully. Their eyes locked. Her arms wrapped around his neck. He moved deep and slow, the tension between them snapping with every thrust.

"I'm yours," she whispered.

He kissed her, hard. "Forever."

After, they redressed in silence. The air between them, electric.

Raygen looked at the dress, still hanging neatly.

Frank picked it up, held it to her chest. "We'll come back for it."

Raygen smirked. "We?"

He kissed her forehead. "It's already yours."

Suddenly, her gaze weakened as she took another look at her reflection in the mirror, returning to the present moment.

A whisper full of passion and confidence escaped her lips. "Yes! I'm yours."

Chapter 14: Back to Where We Began

Raygen had no idea where they were going.

Frank just told her to pack light, bring something soft, something sexy, and something she didn't mind getting wet.

Curious, she raised a brow.

Now, here they were—winding down a private drive lined with trees that parted to reveal a sleek glass lake villa. Flat roof. Floor-to-ceiling windows. Clean lines. Light wood against black stone. Every inch whispered modern luxury with a hint of retreat.

Raygen stepped out of the car, her heels sinking into the gravel. "Where are we?"

Frank smiled. "A soft place to land."

She looked around, stunned. The lake shimmered in the distance. A private dock jutted out like it was made for their silhouettes. Inside, the house gleamed, sunlight bouncing off white oak floors and concrete counters.

Minimalist, but warm. Open, but intimate.

Raygen wandered, taking it all in.

"It's like a rich version of Saint Thomas," she whispered.

Frank came up behind her, sliding his arms around her waist. "I wanted to bring you back to where it started. Just us. Before the noise. Before the work. Just the feeling."

They made the place their own instantly.

Raygen wrapped herself in a cream robe and moved barefoot through the space. Frank poured wine and pulled her onto the couch, her legs across his lap. They didn't talk about the residency. Or business. Or the past.

They talked travel.

Dreams.

What kind of furniture they'd pick for their first real home together.

What their Sundays would feel like.

That night, Frank led her to the oversized soaking tub facing the lake. Candles glowed on every ledge. Music pulsed low in the background.

Raygen slid into the hot water with a sigh, her eyes fluttering shut.

Frank joined, knees brushing hers.

No words.

Just the lake outside.

Steam rising.

And his hand tracing slow circles on her thigh.

He kissed her shoulder. Then her neck. Then her jaw.

"I'm still in love with you," he whispered.

Raygen turned to face him, straddled him in the water, her hands on his cheeks. "Then show me."

He did.

In the water.

On the cool marble of the bathroom floor.

Later, in bed, with her legs wrapped tight around him, her name poured from his lips like a promise.

They didn't rush.

Every stroke was a conversation.

Every kiss, a full sentence.

Every moan, a shared vow.

The next morning, sunlight spilled through the windows.

Raygen moved through the house in one of Frank's T-shirts, her hair wild, her skin glowing.

She found it taped to the inside of the fridge:

"Read this when you're alone."

She peeled it off, opened the folded paper.

Ray,
I don't need an island to feel peace.
I just need you.
I built this trip from a memory,
but what I really want
is to build a life from this moment.
When you go to New York, I'll hold it
down.
But when you come back—
come back ready.
Ready to choose this.
Ready to choose us.
Always,
—F

Raygen clutched the letter to her chest, heart swelling.
The villa. The view. The feeling.
This wasn't just a getaway.
It was a prelude.

Chapter 15: First Class Forever

"You're sure this isn't a setup?" Raygen asked, eyeing the sleek black car waiting outside their building.

Frank smirked as he closed her carry-on. "I told you—it's business. Quick turnaround. I just want you with me."

She raised an eyebrow. "Since when do you fly me out for board meetings?"

"Since I'm tired of sleeping without you."

He leaned in, kissed her forehead. "Besides, we got some celebrating to do. Project's fully funded. Six-Figure Starters is about to hit the next level."

Raygen's eyes softened. "That's big."

"You're bigger," he said, opening the door for her. "Now come on. Wheels up in an hour."

They arrived at O'Hare just in time for a smooth pull-up to the private terminal.

Raygen squinted. "Why is the plane so… quiet?"

Frank slid his sunglasses down. "'Cause it's ours for the day."

Before she could protest, the flight attendant greeted them with a warm smile and two glasses of champagne.

Raygen stepped into the cabin, eyes widening.

Cream leather seats. Rose petals near the window. A tray of chocolate-dipped fruit already waiting.

And at the far end?

A window seat marked with a small brass plaque.

Seat 4F.

She turned slowly, heart pounding. "Frank…"

He set their bags down, took her hand. "Just felt like the right seat for you."

Once they were in the air, the mood shifted.

Raygen curled up in the window seat with her legs tucked beneath her, sipping champagne and watching the clouds roll by. Frank sat across from her, his laptop open but untouched.

He was watching her.

"You good?" he asked, voice low.

She nodded. "It's peaceful up here. Like everything makes sense."

He closed the laptop. "That's how I feel every time I

look at you."

Midway through the flight, the attendant returned with a small velvet box on a silver tray.

Raygen looked at it, confused. "That's... not dessert."

Frank stood slowly.

Cleared his throat.

"Raygen Elise Porter."

Her eyes shot up to his, full, and wet before he even got the box open.

"I met you in this seat. On a random flight that changed everything."

He knelt in front of her, seatbelt sign be damned.

"I didn't know I was sitting next to my future. I didn't know a woman could challenge me, calm me, excite me, and hold me down—all at once."

He opened the box.

A simple, radiant band with a pear-cut stone that sparkled perfectly.

"I've built a lot of things. But this—you—are the only legacy I give a damn about."

"Frank..." she whispered.

"I want to build a life where you never have to question if you're safe, if you're seen, or if you're loved. I want to sit beside you through every flight, every fight, every soft landing. Marry me, baby. Be my forever seatmate."

She covered her mouth, tears falling freely now.

Then nodded.

"Yes," she breathed. "Yes! Yes! Yes!"

He slipped the ring on her finger and stood, pulling her up with him.

They kissed, deep and unapologetically, the plane still gliding steadily through the clouds.

Later, they lay tangled in the back cabin, his shirt half-open, her silk blouse somewhere on the floor.

"You do realize we're engaged now," she whispered against his chest.

"I do," he said. "And when we land, I'm booking our honeymoon—just don't tell my assistant."

Raygen smiled, tracing his jaw with her finger. "I can't believe it started with one seat."

Frank looked at her, eyes full.

"It started with you."

Chapter 16: The Engagement High

The minute Raygen stepped through her front door, her phone lit up like it had been waiting for her to breathe.

37 unread messages. 22 missed calls. 6 voicemails.

She didn't even bother unlocking it. Just turned to Frank and said, "I think they know."

Frank followed her inside, setting their bags down with a soft thud. "If that flight attendant posted what I think she did, we might be trending."

Raygen raised an eyebrow. "You're joking."

He pulled out his phone, swiped, and showed her.

Sure enough—there it was. A photo of Frank, down on one knee in front of seat 4F, smiling up at her with all the intention in the world. Champagne flutes in the background. Her hand halfway to her mouth in shock.

"Real love, real altitude. #Seat4F #BlackLove"

Her chest fluttered again, like it did when it actually

happened.

"Well," she said with a grin, "I guess it's really real now."

The calls and text messages started coming in nonstop.

First it was Jasmyn.

"Raygen Elise Porter. If you do not answer this phone, I will show up to your building barefoot in a bonnet."

Raygen laughed, picked up, and switched to video call. "You happy now?"

Jasmyn's scream was so loud, Frank winced from across the room.

"Let me see the ring! Move your hand slower! Slower!"

Raygen showed off her finger with a soft, glowing smile.

"You better marry that man and let me plan the bachelorette trip," Jasmyn said, already texting someone in the background.

Frank yelled from the kitchen, "No Vegas!"

Jasmyn rolled her eyes. "Y'all so soft now. Ugh. I love it."

An hour later, there was a knock at the door.

Raygen opened it and blinked. "Aunt Netta?"

Frank's aunt stepped in like she paid the mortgage, holding a bottle of champagne in one hand and a white box in the other.

"Y'all didn't think I was gon' let this engagement go down without toasting, did you?"

"Auntie, how did you even know—" Frank started, but Netta cut him off with a look.

"I got eyes everywhere, baby. And a good friend at O'Hare who knows how to mind my business."

She walked straight to the kitchen, set the bottle on the counter, and pulled out two crystal flutes from the cabinet like she lived there. Then turned and pointed at Frank with mock sternness.

"And don't be actin' brand new now that you got your fine self a fiancée. I was holding it down when you were broke and heartbroken."

Raygen raised an eyebrow, amused. "Heartbroken?"

Frank groaned. "Here we go…"

Aunt Netta grinned wide, already pouring champagne. "Mmhmm. Little Frankie used to come lay on my couch talkin' 'bout how he wasn't gon' ever trust another woman. Swore off dating, remember that?"

Frank shook his head, laughing. "I was twenty-three. You told me I needed therapy and a haircut."

"And I was right about both," she said, handing him a glass. "But look at you now. Billionaire with a backbone and a Black queen on his arm. I'm proud of you, nephew."

Frank's expression softened. "You helped me believe I could have more."

Aunt Netta touched his cheek. "You were always gon' have more. You just had to see it first."

Raygen watched the exchange with quiet warmth, heart expanding. She had grown up with her Aunt Vi treating her the same way.

With the day ending, and the door finally closed behind their visitors, the apartment grew still again.

Raygen collapsed onto the couch with a groan. "That was a lot."

Frank sat beside her, unbuttoning the top of his shirt. "You good?"

She turned to him. "I am. A little overwhelmed, but… it's a good overwhelmed."

He nodded. "Yeah."

A pause passed between them—quiet but full.

Raygen laid her head on his shoulder, then asked softly, "What kind of wedding do you want?"

Frank let the question settle before answering. "Honestly? I just want you at the end of the aisle. You could be in a courthouse dress or something lacy with all the extras. I don't care. I just want it to be us."

Raygen turned her face toward him. "You think we should write our own vows?"

"I think we already have," he said, kissing her slow.

They didn't have sex that night.

They didn't need to.

Their intimacy was in the ease of shared silence, in the weight of her head on his chest, in the way his hand never left her thigh.

Everything else could wait.

But this—

This was forever.

Chapter 17: Bridal, Bougie & Boundaries

Raygen stared at the text from Jasmyn.

"Group chat meets real life: today @ noon. Bridal brunch. No excuses. Wear white. 💍✨ "

She rolled her eyes playfully and typed back:

"I' m literally still recovering from the last group scream session. Do I need heels?"

Jasmyn:

"Absolutely! You' re a fiancée now. Click clack or don' t come. "

They met at a private loft Jasmyn had rented for the afternoon. Sunlight streamed through floor-to-ceiling windows. The whole place smelled of peonies and fresh fruit. Gold-rimmed glasses sparkled next to plates of lemon ricotta pancakes and mimosas lined up like soldiers.

Raygen walked in wearing a simple white jumpsuit and soft curls pinned to one side.

"Okay, okay," someone said. "She's giving elegant fiancée energy!"

"Right? Like a grown woman with a trust fund she built herself!"

Raygen laughed and hugged each woman—old colleagues, a cousin from Atlanta, a friend from a women's entrepreneurship group. Everyone hugged her like she was the prize… and in that moment, she believed it.

Brunch buzzed with energy.

Jasmyn pulled out swatches and said, "Okay, so what are we thinking? Garden glam? West Side rooftop? Destination chic?"

Raygen sipped her drink. "I'm thinking… not sure yet. Can I just say 'intentional luxury' and let y'all do the rest?"

"Intentional luxury," Jasmyn repeated, writing it down. "I can work with that."

Everyone giggled.

But Raygen's smile dimmed a little.

Because between the laughter, the floral arrangements, and the cake tasting conversation, something crept in.

She didn't know what it was at first.

But when one of the women said, "You're so lucky—he chose you," it hit.

That old feeling.

That lie she used to carry like a purse with broken straps.

Lucky.

Like love was something she stumbled upon. Like she hadn't done the work. Like she wasn't the one who chose, too.

Raygen blinked and looked down at her ring.

It sparkled just fine.

But for a moment, her heart didn't.

Jasmyn pulled her aside near the bar, reading her like only a best friend could.

"You good?"

Raygen nodded slowly. "Yeah. Just tired."

Jasmyn leaned in. "No, you not. Talk to me."

Raygen sighed. "I don't like when people say I'm lucky. I didn't fall into Frank. I chose him. We built this. It wasn't magic."

Jasmyn nodded. "Say that."

"I worked hard to become the version of me that could receive love like this."

"You earned it, Ray. Period."

Raygen exhaled.

Then smiled. "You always know how to bring me back."

"Of course. That's what maids of honor do."

Raygen blinked. "Wait—did you just name yourself?"

Jasmyn shrugged. "You already knew."

They both laughed.

By the time she left, Raygen felt lighter. Her girls had ideas, vision boards, and shade for days. But more than that—they had her back.

She walked out of the loft into the late afternoon sun, heels clicking on concrete, a new mantra forming beneath her breath:

I'm not lucky.

I'm aligned.

Chapter 18: Meet Me at the Manor

Frank didn't give her much to go on.

Just a "be ready by 2" and a "wear something soft."

Raygen showed up in a cream knit dress and gold hoops, curious but unbothered. Their post-engagement glow hadn't worn off yet, and she was riding it like sunlight on a warm day.

The driver pulled up in front of a tall, black wrought-iron gate, lined with ivy and trimmed hedges. Beyond it stood a brick mansion—wide, regal, and black as ever.

"Where are we?" she asked, stepping out as Frank opened her door.

He grinned. "Black Women in Leadership Historic. Fully restored. Former Black-owned estate turned private event space… with a waiting list two years long."

Raygen blinked. "And yet… we're here?"

"I know people," he said, smug. "And I wrote a check."

They walked the grounds first.

The gravel crunched beneath their shoes as Frank led her around manicured lawns and through tall oaks swaying like elders. A wraparound porch curled around the main house, and tucked behind it was a courtyard with a small koi pond and a stone path leading to a detached glass greenhouse.

Raygen touched Frank's arm. "It feels... sacred."

"That's what I thought, too."

They stepped inside next—exposed beams, grand staircase, rich oak floors that whispered legacy with every step. The dining room held portraits of Black families who once dined there. The library still smelled of mahogany and oil. It wasn't just a house—it was a museum of memory.

In the sitting room, light spilled across a velvet settee. Frank turned to her.

"I thought this could be our venue. Or... our future."

Raygen looked up sharply. "Wait, what?"

"It's for sale. Quiet deal. The board's picky, but they respect legacy buyers. Folks who won't flip it or water it down. I gave them our names."

She stared at him. "You're serious."

"I'm always serious about you."

They sat for a moment on the window bench, just beyond the sun flare. Raygen couldn't stop touching the old carved wood, couldn't stop picturing things:

The smell of food. Her cousins laughing in the hallway. A summer party out back with jazz playing loud and drinks sweating on the table. Maybe even... a little girl with Frank's smile and her stubbornness, climbing those stairs barefoot.

Then she blinked. "Wait—what about the blueprints?"

Frank laughed under his breath. "I was just about to say that."

They both smiled, shaking their heads.

"We were gonna build from the ground up," Raygen said.

"We still could," Frank replied. "But this... this feels like it already has our name in the walls."

Raygen looked around again, slower this time.

"I love it here."

"I knew you would."

They walked the grounds one more time, hand in hand.

And as they passed beneath the arched iron gate, she paused.

Turned to him.

"Let's do it," she said.

He raised a brow. "The wedding? The house?"

"All of it."

Chapter 19: The Softest Yes

The bridal suite was quiet.

Not silent—there was soft music playing somewhere, the gentle sweep of fabric, the distant rustle of people arriving—but quiet in the way a heart feels before something sacred.

Raygen sat alone by the arched window, the sunlight laying across her bare shoulders. Her wedding dress hung on the door, but she hadn't reached for it yet. She wasn't stalling—just... soaking.

A year ago, she didn't know love could look like this. Didn't know it could be both soft and certain. Saint Thomas changed her, sure. But it was everything after— the arguments, the vulnerability, the holding each other down when the pressure got public—that turned this love into something real.

"Knock, knock," Jasmyn said, slipping in and closing the door behind her.

Raygen looked up. "You good?"

Jasmyn grinned. "Girl, I came to ask you that."

They hugged, a long, swaying kind of hug; then relaxed their embrace. When they pulled apart, Jasmyn said, "You remember that dude you dated who had the nerve to bring you gas station flowers and ask to borrow your car?"

Raygen laughed, "Please don't bring him up on my wedding day."

"I just need to say this," Jasmyn said, suddenly serious. "I watched you settle so many times. But this time? You chose something that feels like it was made for you. And I'm proud of you."

Raygen's eyes watered. "Thank you. That means more than you know."

"Now put on that damn dress," Jasmyn said, smirking. "And let this man see what he prayed for."

Across the manor, Frank stood at the altar on the back lawn.

He looked good—sharp black tux, low fade clean, hands folded but steady. Guests whispering, taking pictures, wiping tears, dabbing sweat. But he only had space in his mind for one person.

Aunt Netta stepped up beside him and adjusted his boutonnière with a soft fuss.

"You ever seen your mama this morning?" she

asked.

Frank smiled. "In my dreams."

"Well, she's here now. Don't need to see her to know that."

She patted his chest. "She'd be proud of the man you are. And of the woman you chose."

"I'm proud too," he said quietly. "Grateful."

Aunt Netta leaned in closer. "You ready to love her when it's not magical? When it's not sexy? When it's just bills and family stuff and 'what's for dinner'?"

"Yes, Ma'am."

"Good. Then she's already won."

The music changed.

Everyone stood.

Raygen stepped out onto the grass with her arm linked in her cousin Marcus's. She'd asked him last minute— someone who'd seen her through childhood, heartbreak, and hustle.

"You good?" he whispered.

She nodded, lips tight. "Just keep me from floating off."

The walk felt longer than it looked. Her heartbeat thumped in her ears. But the moment she locked eyes with Frank, the world quieted.

Every step pulled her closer to a man who had seen

her—in all her light and all her shadow—and never blinked.

They stood facing each other, hands locked.

Frank spoke first.

"I knew I loved you when you tried to act like Saint Thomas was just a vacation. When you kissed me like a secret and laughed like you didn't need saving. But I wanted to stay. Not just in the sun, but in your storm."

Raygen swallowed. Her voice trembled when she spoke.

"I used to think peace was for other people. That I had to be hard to survive, to earn love. But then you showed up. Patient. Steady. You didn't fix me—you waited for me to heal and offered your shoulder while I did."

They both smiled through misty eyes.

"I vow to love you when it's loud," she said, "and when it's quiet."

"I vow to protect your heart," he replied, "even when I don't understand it."

"I vow to choose you," they said together, "again and again."

When they kissed, the crowd exhaled like they'd all been holding their breath.

A little girl in the second row clapped with her whole

body. An older couple held hands tighter. Jasmyn was sobbing silently. Aunt Netta closed her eyes, head bowed as if she was in prayer.

The reception was already alive with music and champagne, but Frank only had eyes for Raygen.

He pulled her close during their first dance and whispered, "Still want that custom house?"

Raygen leaned her head against his chest. "We've already built something better."

Later, while folks were dancing, he tugged her hand and slipped away from the crowd.

They kissed under the stars behind the manor; her dress rustling like wind through trees, his hands secure on her waist.

"I'll never get tired of this," she whispered.

Frank's lips brushed her ear. "I've wanted you since the second you boarded the plane and sat in seat 4F."

"And now?" she asked, breathless.

"Now you're mine."

Frank led her through a side door in a quiet area of the manor and up the stairs into a private room.

Her dress whispered against the hardwood as he backed her toward the bed, her laugh caught in his mouth, her hands already pulling at his tie.

His hands slid down her hips, slowly and reverently,

like he was relearning every inch. She peeled his shirt away and kissed across his chest—soft, then deeper. He lifted her in one motion, laying her down on satin sheets, her thighs trembling beneath his palms.

They moved like memory and music.

Like nothing existed but the press of skin and the rhythm only they knew.

He worshipped her with his mouth, her body arching under the heat of it. She pulled him deeper with her thighs, dragging her nails across his back. He groaned low, then fell silent—holding her eyes as he slid inside her with slow, deliberate control.

Raygen gasped, forehead pressed to his. "This…this is what love feels like."

Frank gripped her tighter. "This is what we feel like."

They didn't stop when the climax hit.

They just moved slower, sweeter—two souls making a promise with their bodies.

Afterward, they lay tangled in sheets and moonlight, her legs draped over his, his chest rising beneath her cheek.

Nothing rushed.

Nothing broken.

Just everything they ever needed… in one room, in one night.

Chapter 20: Seat 4F – Full Circle

Morning in Chicago.

No filters. No fanfare.

Just sunlight creeping through the bay window, warming the hardwood floor and touching Raygen's bare shoulders as she sat curled in her favorite spot. Coffee in one hand, peace in the other.

She wore one of Frank's T-shirts, oversized and warm with his scent, her wedding band glinting in the light like it knew it had stories to tell.

No rush.

No makeup.

No flight to catch.

Just this moment—and the quiet power of being chosen.

Frank padded into the room, shirtless and barefoot, rubbing sleep from his eyes.

"You good?" he asked.

Raygen didn't even turn around. "Mmhm."

He came up behind her, wrapped his arms around her middle, and kissed the curve of her neck.

"You sure?"

She leaned into him. "I'm really married to you?"

"Whole thing's legal. Too late now."

She laughed, soft and real. "It still feels like a dream."

"Feels like we earned this dream," he said, resting his chin on her shoulder. "Piece by piece."

They sat like that for a while.

No words.

Just two hearts in sync.

And then—

A knock at the door.

Raygen glanced over her shoulder. "You expecting someone?"

Frank shook his head. "We got security. Who gets past that?"

Raygen pulled on a robe, padded over to the door, and opened it slowly.

A young woman stood there—no more than twenty-three, maybe twenty-four—wearing a blazer and nervous energy.

"Hi," she said. "Sorry to just show up. Are you Raygen Porter?"

Raygen blinked. "Yes?"

The woman smiled, small but certain. "You started that entrepreneurship program last fall... the one that helps young adults build six-figure businesses?"

Raygen nodded, confused.

"I was in your first cohort," she said. "And I just hit my first $100K. I bought my mom a car last week. And I just... I needed to thank you. In person."

Raygen's throat tightened.

Frank stepped up beside her. "You came all the way here to say that?"

The young woman gazed at the pair. "You two changed my life."

Raygen opened the door wider. "Come in."

The girl stepped inside, eyes wide as she took in the space. "It's even more beautiful than I imagined."

Raygen smiled. "So are you."

Later, when the girl left, Raygen stood in the middle of the living room and turned to Frank.

"This is why we work," she said. "Not just 'cause we're in love. But because we give it back."

Frank nodded. "Love and legacy. That was always the blueprint."

Raygen walked back to her seat by the window, picked up her tea, and looked out at the sky.

Her phone buzzed.

An invite to speak at a national summit.

A message from Zeven about expanding the program.

An email with the subject: **Mrs. Sheldon – Deed Confirmation.**

She closed it all.

Looked up.

Smiled.

And whispered, "Seat 4F really was the beginning."

Frank sat beside her, taking her hand.

"Nah," he said. "This right here? This is where we take off."

Bonus Epilogue: Return Flight

Three months later.

Private terminal. Just before sunrise.

Raygen stood on the tarmac, caramel trench belted at the waist, steam rising from her tea. Her curls, tucked under a silk wrap, and her eyes fixed on the sleek jet in front of her.

Frank approached, behind her, rolling both carry-ons like it were second nature.

"You good?"

She turned and grinned. "You really flying me out before 6 a.m. with no itinerary?"

He leaned in, brushed a kiss along her jaw. "Trust me. This one's worth it."

Raygen's phone buzzed in her coat pocket.

She pulled it out, thumb hovering before unlocking it. One new message:

"Hi Ms. Raygen. Just got the confirmation that I was accepted to the DC Women's Summit. Thank you for submitting my name. I never saw this path for myself before your program. Now I can't unsee it. 🙏✨" —J. Parks

Raygen stared at the message, heart swelling.

Frank noticed her pause. "You good?"

She looked over at him, eyes full.

"I really am."

They boarded without a word to the staff. No fanfare. No distractions.

Just them.

The cabin was plush, quiet, and warmly lit—private like a whisper. Champagne chilled in the corner. A familiar scent clung to the air: sandalwood and something sweet.

Raygen slid into her seat.

Then froze.

Seat 4F.

She ran her hand over the stitched leather and looked over at Frank, already lounging across from her with that smug smile.

"You customized the jet?"

He nodded once. "Had to keep the energy aligned."

She laughed, touched to her core. "This is wild."

Frank reached into his inside pocket, pulled out a slim envelope, and handed it to her.

Inside: a deed.

Not to the house.

Not to the manor.

But to the West Side building they'd bought months ago—the one she'd dreamed of transforming into a flagship training center for their entrepreneurship program.

She looked up, stunned.

"You bought it out?"

He nodded again, this time softer. "For you. For the kids who need it. For every version of you who thought they had to make it alone."

Her chest tightened. She didn't even try to blink the tears away.

He reached for her hand, squeezing it gently. "You good?"

She smiled slowly, letting it sit in her bones.

"I'm about to be."

Later, after champagne kisses and whispered plans for the future, they curled up on the wide leather couch near the window. Raygen lay across Frank's chest, skin warm beneath a silk blanket.

The world felt still up here. Elevated.

His fingers traced the curve of her back.

Raygen exhaled, eyes fluttering closed. "Frank…"

"Yeah?"

"I think we're finally flying the way we were meant to."

He kissed the top of her head.

"Welcome to your forever flight."

The End.